The Wiggles

A Very Wiggly Christmas

ISBN 0-448-43424-5   A B C D E F G H I J

The Wiggles

A Very Wiggly Christmas

**Illustrated by
Bob Berry Illustration**

Grosset & Dunlap

It was Christmas Eve and Santa came to visit. "One of my reindeer is sick," he told The Wiggles sadly. "It takes the whole team to pull my sleigh. I'm afraid I can't deliver my Christmas presents."

The Wiggles knew what it was like to be a team. "Trying to sing without one of us would be like driving on three tires," Anthony said. Then he snapped his fingers. "That's it! We can make your Christmas deliveries in our Big Red Car."

"Yeah!" agreed Greg. "The Big Red Car always gets us where we need to go."

"Let's go!" Jeff yawned. Then he fell asleep!

"Wake up, Jeff!" The Wiggles shouted.

Jeff opened his eyes. "A Christmas morning without a visit from Santa just isn't Christmas. Let's get wiggling!"

So with a vroom-vroom and a happy
song, The Wiggles and Santa took off
in the Big Red Car full of Santa's gifts.

Everywhere they went, The Wiggles found people
wiggling with Christmas Eve glee. When the Car
touched down in Italy, the children danced a tarantella.
The dance was so much fun, even Santa joined in!
While he was busy, The Wiggles delivered lots of
gifts—and Anthony ate many delicious Italian
Christmas cookies.

When the Car touched down in London,
The Wiggles saw children dancing so fast,
their feet barely touched the ground.

When the Big Red Car landed in Ireland, The Wiggles saw children bouncing up and down.
"Are you all wiggling for Christmas?" Greg asked.
The children nodded. "We're dancing a jig for joy!"

When they arrived in Scotland, they saw that everyone was dancing there, too!

"I guess the whole world is wiggling with excitement over Christmas," Anthony said.

Jeff yawned. "It makes me look forward to my Christmas Day nap," he said, closing his eyes.

"Wake up, Jeff!" The Wiggles said. "There's still plenty of dancing and deliveries to do."

"And holiday cookies to eat!" Anthony added.

In New York, the kids danced the funky monkey. "There's nothing like Yuletide wiggling!" the children told The Wiggles.

"If you can wiggle here, you can wiggle anywhere!" one said.
So Santa and The Wiggles wiggled, too.

Then the Big Red Car took off again.
This time it landed in Argentina, where the
children were dancing the tango to celebrate
the holidays.

When all the presents were delivered,
The Wiggles headed home to Australia.
They wanted to spend Christmas Eve with
their families and friends.

Wags the Dog was so happy to see
them, he did a cartwheel for joy!

Dorothy the Dinosaur and Henry the Octopus had missed The Wiggles, too.

"Welcome home!" they said. "We hope you had a good time spreading holiday cheer around the world."

"It was the best Christmas Eve ever!" Greg told Dorothy the Dinosaur. "I'm so happy that we could help Santa deliver his presents to the good boys and girls all over the world."

Dorothy nodded her head in agreement.
It really had been a wonderful Christmas Eve.

Santa was grateful to The Wiggles for all their
help. "Ho, ho, ho! You're the wiggliest helpers I
ever had. And this was the best Christmas Eve.
I'd like to reward you with a song."

Suddenly, sweetly singing angels surrounded The Wiggles.

When the song was over, Murray sighed. "That was the most beautiful Christmas carol I've ever heard." "What a beautiful present," said Greg.

"We should give something to Santa, too!" Anthony added.

Jeff stretched and yawned. "But what? None of the stores are open." Then he closed his eyes.

"Wake up, Jeff!" Greg shouted. "We have to make Santa a gift."

Just then, Captain Feathersword walked by with an armload of tinsel. The friendly pirate always decorated his tree at the last minute.

Anthony snapped his fingers. Then he whispered to the captain.

The pirate burst into a hearty laugh. "Arr! Well, deck the halls! I'd be happy to be a gift for Santa." So The Wiggles put all the decorations on Captain Feathersword. Soon, the pirate looked as festive as the finest Christmas tree.

The Wiggles presented their "tree" to Santa.
"Ho, ho, ho!" Santa chuckled. "This is the most
original Christmas present I have ever received.
But I don't need a gift. Helping me save Christmas
is the best gift you could've given . . ."

". . . in fact, having you and your friends around
has made this Christmas perfectly. . . wiggly!"
And, with that, Santa started to dance.

Santa and The Wiggles
want you to have a very
wiggly Christmas, too!